Banana Monster

Peter Bently

QED Publishing

Charlie was telling his baby brother Chester a story about monsters.

"Monsters are huge and scary!" said Charlie.

"Oo-ooh!" said Chester. "I hope I never meet one!"

"Silly little Chester," chuckled Charlie. "Fancy believing in monsters!"

"Now, I feel peckish. Time to visit my secret stash of bananas!"

Charlie crept through the bushes. Then he stopped.

"Uh-oh. What was that noise?"

He could hear someone eating his bananas!

"Eek!"

cried Charlie.
"It must be... a

monster!"

Charlie ran back home to his mum.

"What's the matter?" asked Mum.

"I think there's a **monster** in the bushes!" said Charlie.

"There aren't any monsters in the forest, Charlie," said Mum kindly.

"Come on, let's go and see."

Suddenly they heard a loud grunting sound.

"It's the monster!" shivered Charlie. "Asleep in the bushes!"

"Why don't you climb that tree and look?" said Mum. "You'll be safe up there."

Quietly as a mouse,
Charlie started to climb.

Carefully...

does...

it.

Just a little closer...

At last Charlie
looked down into
the bushes and saw...

the monster!

It was Chester – asleep after eating all Charlie's bananas!

Notes for parents and teachers

• Before reading the book with a child, or children, look at the cover and see if they can think what the story is about.

• Read the story aloud to the child or children. Encourage them to join in with any animal noises. Can they guess what happens in the end? Which pictures do they like best?

• In the story, Charlie tells his baby brother Chester a scary story about monsters. Ask the children to explain, in their own words, how Chester ends up scaring Charlie.

• Have the children ever seen a real chimpanzee? Chimps are our closest relatives in the animal world. How are they similar to humans, and how are they different? Discuss where chimps live and what they like to eat.

• Make the story of Charlie and Chester into a play. One child can be Charlie and two others can play Chester and Mum. The rest of the children can be other chimps or different jungle animals – or the monsters that Charlie imagines.

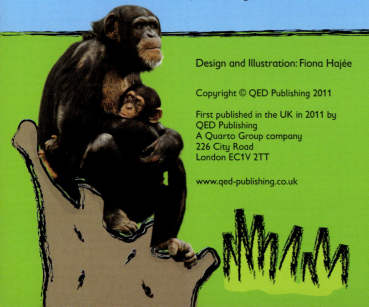

Design and Illustration: Fiona Hajée

Copyright © QED Publishing 2011

First published in the UK in 2011 by
QED Publishing
A Quarto Group company
226 City Road
London EC1V 2TT

www.qed-publishing.co.uk

A catalogue record for this book is available from the British Library.

ISBN 978 1 84835 644 3

Printed in China

Picture credits (t=top, b=bottom, l=left, r=right, c=centre)
FLPA front cover Cyril Ruoso/Minden Pictures, 1 Jurgen & Christine Sohns, 2 Fritz Polking, 3 Cyril Ruoso/Minden Pictures, 4 & 5 Jurgen & Christine Sohns, 8 Suzi Eszterhas/Minden Pictures, 10 Gerard Lacz, 12–13 & 14–15 Jurgen & Christine Sohns, 16–17 Terry Whittaker, 18l and 18r Cyril Ruoso/Minden Pictures, 21 Frans Lanting, 22 Cyril Ruoso/Minden Pictures, 24 Terry Whittaker
Nature Picture Library 7 Andy Rouse, 19 Suzi Eszterhas
Shutterstock back cover Eric Isselée